# How I breathe

First published in the U.S. in 1992 by Carolrhoda Books, Inc.

Library of Congress Cataloging-in-Publication Data

Suhr, Mandy.
    How I breathe / by Mandy Suhr; illustrated by Mike Gordon.
        p.   cm. – (I'm alive)
    Summary: A simple explanation of how people, animals, and
plants breathe.
    ISBN 0-87614-736-8 (lib. bdg.)
    1. Respiration–Juvenile literature. [1. Respiration.] I. Gordon,
Mike, ill. II. Title. III. Series: Suhr, Mandy. I'm alive.
QP121.S86  1992
574.1'2–dc20                                              91-36753
                                                              CIP
                                                              AC

Printed in Belgium by Casterman, S.A.
Bound in the United States of America

1  2  3  4  5  6  7  8  9  10  01  00  99  98  97  96  95  94  93  92

# How I breathe

written by Mandy Suhr

illustrated by Mike Gordon

I'm alive!

■ Carolrhoda Books, Inc./Minneapolis

When I was a tiny baby inside my mommy, she breathed for both of us.

As soon as I was born, I started to breathe on my own. I am breathing all the time.

People and most other animals breathe air. We can't see or feel air, but it is all around us.

One of the gases in the air is called oxygen. Oxygen makes my muscles work.

When I breathe in air through my nose and mouth, the oxygen begins its journey to my muscles.

The air goes down a pipe and into my lungs. My lungs take the oxygen out of the air and send it into my blood.

My blood carries the oxygen around my body to all my muscles.

9

The parts of air that I don't
need are pushed out of my lungs,
back up the pipe, and out of my
nose and mouth.

As I breathe in and my lungs fill with air, my chest gets bigger.

As I breathe out, my chest gets smaller again.

Sometimes when I'm running or playing soccer, my muscles need to work harder. They need more oxygen!

Then I have to breathe faster to get more air into my lungs.

Plants need air too. They breathe through their leaves...

but you can't see them breathing.

Plants don't have muscles that need oxygen. But they do need other gases in the air to help them grow.

Most animals breathe air the same way that we do.  Stan, my dog, needs oxygen for his muscles just as I do.

Fish don't breathe air,
but they do need oxygen.
They have a special way of
breathing.  They take oxygen
from the water that they live in.

19

Breathing isn't always easy.
Dirty or smoky air makes our
lungs dirty. Then they don't
work as well.

Dirty air clogs up plants' leaves.
If they can't breathe, they die.

Can you name these
things that make
our air dirty?

Here are a few ways to
keep our air clean–and
make it easier for us
to breathe.

# A note to adults

"I'm Alive" is a series of books designed especially for preschoolers and beginning readers. These books look at how the human body works and develops. They compare the human body to plants and animals that are already familiar to children.

Here are some activities that use what kids already know to learn more about breathing.

## Activities

**1.** Blow up a balloon. Watch how it gets bigger as you fill it with air. Your lungs are like two balloons. They get bigger as they fill up with air. Can you feel your chest filling up with air as you breathe in?

**2.** Have someone time you as you do jumping jacks for one minute. Then try it for two minutes, and then three minutes. What happens to your breathing after each time?

**3.** When air has become dirty, we say it's polluted. Find pictures in magazines or newspapers of things that pollute the air. Draw pictures. Put all of these pictures on one half of a poster. Now find pictures of things that don't pollute for the other half.

**4.** Do you know someone with a fish tank? What do you think happens if the water gets dirty and no one cleans the tank? The fish die. The same thing happens in lakes, rivers, and ponds. When people dump poisons and garbage in the water, the fish can't breathe and they die. Next time you go to a lake or river or pond, you can help the fish by picking up any garbage you see lying within your reach.

24